"Reaven - Legend of Isara"

Acknowledgments

First I would have to thank my lord and savior Jesus Christ for blessing me and giving me the opportunity to share my gift with the world. To my family Tamara "Sista" Morales and my two beautiful nieces Savanna and Leanna Hartfield I love you. Thank you to all my friends who supported me in this endevour I love you and appreciate you!

Special thanks to everyone who purchased the book

Preface

Indescribable pain as I felt my rib cage rip in desolate places outside my chest. My bones were being crushed and turned in every direction imaginable, with no plea loud enough to make it end. Time seemed to stand still as I attempted to scream but eventually my vocal cords ripped apart until I was choking on my own blood. The torment for any Zephyrian would normally last a few moments, but this punishment was Ka-bal's edict to the citizens of Zephyr that his sovereignty would not be defiled. Anguish seeped through my flesh through every body part, even the tips of my hairs screamed to exude this treacherous brutishness that caused my lost tranquility. Ka-bal ensured that I would suffer the greatest demise that was ever bestowed upon on any Zephyrian.

......In my final moment before my passing from this world to the next, the words of the Osawa appeared to me "Your suffering will be legendary" and suddenly my pain was over.... I was dead.

In life, I had very little purpose... In death, I became something much more...

A legend...

Chapter 1

It only took one Agantus to kill Ka-bal's finest warrior. Verdic was the strongest, most feared combatant and overly confident in any battle he pursued. Fear never was apparent when he was in battle and it kept him alive up until now, that same attitude and impulse sent him to the Gregorie head first. Agantus is a massive creature with scales that ran down his back, his mouth split down the middle and when he opened it. It was like looking into a black hole with no end. Its teeth were in three layers on the top and bottom of its mouth, they were unevenly assorted throughout its mouth making him look even more threatening.

Agantus was almost as tall as the pilers that held the arena up. He must have weighed a thousand pounds and his skin was thick equivalent to the finest of metals. All over his body were curved spikes that ran down his back and arms, with razor sharp claws that protruded out of its three fingered hands and toes. His skin color was a faint brown unevenly proportioned with long threats that came from his head replacing where hair normally would be. He existed only to be killer, coming from the lowest pits of Gregorie and Ka-bals pet.

This was Ka-bals doing, his sense of entertainment was to watch the toughest warriors get ripped to shreds in battle in the most excruciating and humiliating manor. Gregorie was not a place you wanted to be, it is a place of torment. When the souls left the body of a Zephyrian and lived a bad life, they were considered "damned" and went there. Stories were passed down throughout Zephyr how desolate and intolerable the Gregorie was, this put fear in the eyes of both old and young alike.

The crowds were roaring, cheering on Agantus who had bit off Verdic's hand, his blood splashed everywhere as if it was a broken facet. A Zephyrians blood was dark black with tiny diamond like substances that glimmered from it. Weleks who were Hunters from other cities in Zephyr would hunt and kill just to shed the blood of a Zephyrian collecting the diamonds and sell it for money. Weleks are very dangerous Zephyrians who were ruthless and would do anything for personal gain.

Verdic knew it was over but in his mind he could not admit it to himself that he was going to die and never see Lavina ever again. Lavina was his first and only love and the reason he was fighting in Ka-bals Arena. King Ka-bal and his evil intentions forced soldiers to fight for his entertainment; he was nothing like his father whose stature was strong and had great integrity which was unseen under any others rule. Kabal was an evil tyrant that enjoyed the decay of his own people but the people still loved him.

Vertic was weary from the frequent pounds of the fist that were slamming against his skull and chest repetitively. Agantus was not even tired or phased by any attempts that Vertic had made and they have been fighting for over an hour. "Come on you son of a bitch" Vertic exclaimed "Im not done yet!" Agantus did not speak words but he did get his point across by howling and growling ferociously. Its voice sent out powerful sound waves that knocked Vertic back smashing his face in the dirt on the Arenas cold hard ground. Vertic was feeling dazed from the rapid blood lost from his half eaten arm. He grabbed his sword and pierced Agantus in his thigh, all this did was piss him off even more. Vertic rolled under Agantus legs and cut the back of his foot, Agantus fell forward and onto his knee. The crowed was cheering this was the moment they have been waiting for. The crowd could care less who would win or lose just as long as someone faced a miraculous and glorious fatality.

Vertic lifted up both his hands as if he already won the fight; he jumped on Agantus back using two daggers to climb all the way to his head. Vertic moved swiftly sliding down its spiky back. Agantus face was nearly touching the ground and then Vertic pounced on its face stabbing Agantus's eye then back flipping off his body. Agantus started to stomp because he was in great pain from being impaled. Vertic held his hand and tried to cover it with the cloth that Lavina had given him a long time ago.

Agantus regained his composure, he started howling and growling again until the growls became a loud snarl. He spit out poison from his mouth that Vertic barley dodged. The drool from Agantus lips fell on Vertic's half eaten arm and the poisonous effects started happening immediately. Vertic was beginning to feel numb and his legs began to become weak. He looked over to see Lavina crying out to him telling him to forfeit the fight, she would rather have a half-eaten Vertic then none at all.

Agantus grabbed Verdic by his head and ate his legs and some of his torso, his insides fell to the ground as he took his final breath. Agantus threw his corpse as if it was garbage that needed to be disposed of. Verdic's body hit the Arenas pilers and his body exploded in many pieces, limbs scattered everywhere getting on some of the crowd. Ka-bal stood up and the crowd got silent, as soon as he showed the approval that he was pleased the crowd began to cheer once again. They threw drinks and food in the air in celebration as if they got a glimpse of Isara.

Tesious who was Ka-bals wife, was the total opposite of what anyone would believe a mate for Ka-bal would be. She was a descendent of the Manaja tribe who were deeply rooted in the strongest sorcery in Zephyr. Tesious family were slaves, they lost their freedom decades ago because of illegal usage of magic for self-gratification. They were later sentence by King Arion to be servants for the next 1000 years available for purchase by the locals. When she saw how Ka-bal set up Vertic and was happy about it, she walked away in tears because she loved both Verdict and Lavina. Ka-bal ordered the mages to focus their magic on Agantus so he would go back to his chamber, the servants quickly started cleaning up all the blood and body parts that were scattered around the arena. Ka-bal spoke to the crowd "It is done the un-defeated Agantus has won once again!!! You may all go home for your king is pleased".

Lavina was in shock she could barely catch her breath and it was hard for her to walk or even think clearly. The image of Vertic's death replayed over and over as if it was the only memory she ever had in her head. Ka-bal approached her and apologized to her "I did not know that he was going to face Agantus on his own, I tried to stop him but he insisted that he wanted to show you his love and strength by facing the most powerful of creatures so that he could prove his love to you".

Lavina broke down to her knees she cried but no sound came out. Her throat became dry and closed making it hard for her to grasp what Ka-bal was saying. It was too much for one person to conceive all at once. Her whole life was wiped away as if it was excrement from the bottom of a shoe. She began to sweat profusely and her body was damp and wet as if she ran a marathon, Images of what transpired before her eyes began to replay continuously. Vertic was no longer amongst the living, he was dead and she would never hear his sweet words or kiss him or touch him ever again.

Ka-bal told her that he could reverse what had happened to Vertic and she could see him again. Lavina stopped crying for a moment and opened her eyes "What are you saying?" she said "I know a Mage with great abilities that practices the art of necromancy which retrieves souls that have left this world and entered the next". Lavina said "Please take me to him I need to see Vertic" Ka- bal grinned and put his hand on her shoulder then he told her to follow him, Lavina quickly composed herself and went with Ka-bal to the Mage's tower.

Nexius was one of the most dedicated workers of magic, he could emulate almost any spell at any moment with little to no practice. He was 396 years old quite young for someone who practices magic at the magnitude that he practices. He learned it from his father who was great in sorcery and conjuring spells. His name was Charus and he was a very gifted necromancer and spell caster, he died when Nexius was just 73 years old from consuming high quantities of magic at one time. He became addicted to gaining power and it took over him.

Ka-bal told Lavina to wait outside until he spoke with Nexius, Ka- bal spoke quietly to Nexius so Lavina could not hear what was being said. "Were going to play a little game, I want her to experience what Vertic's death was like and I want you to reenact it completely   for my personal entertainment" Nexius looked at Ka-bal he was perplexed at his request "Why would you ask of such a thing my lord?"Ka-bal smirked "Because it's fun" he said in a dark tone.

Nexius could not look Lavina in her eyes, she asked him "Will I see my love soon? Can you tell me if he is in Isara? Is he in any pain?" Nexius just walked away to his potions and spell book ignoring all her questions but she was too anxious to notice. Ka-bal sat in a chair in the far corner of the room near the window placing his hand at his temple. Nexius looked over at Lavina and asked her to sit in the middle of the room. "I will get you to Vertic and you will be reunited once again" Nexius said to Lavina. Lavina was enthused and desperate so she naively rushed into the center of the room, her hands were clammy from the constant gripping and clenching she was doing. Her heart raced and she began to become nervous and panicked from both fear and happiness.

Lavina said to Ka-bal "Thank you!!! I am forever in your debt. I will never forget what you have done for us" Ka-bal just smiled as Nexius started his ritual "My lady it is you who I am in debt to. I only wish for your happiness" Lavina did not know what he meant by those words nor did she care, her focus was getting to Vertic. Nexus began to cultivate the spirit of Vertic, he then intensely meditate on the spell. Lavina's eyes turned white and she began to shake; she began to see what Vertics last moments were like as if she was there with him.

In her mind, the room began to disintegrate and she saw Vertic face to face with the Agantus. Hearing Vertic speak "Come on you son of bitch" she yelled "Vertic!!! He's going to kill you please stop!!!" The Aganus bit off his hand. She felt exactly what he felt, her hand disintegrated in to thin air, she began to scream in terror as the blood splattered on the floor, her voice echoed throughout the room. Ka-bal was rejoicing inside his rotten flesh, this was what he was waiting for.

Agantus ripped off Vertic's legs, which meant her legs began to disappear with blood pouring out rapidly. She finally realized it was a setup from Ka-bal, She was in a state of shock and disbelief why would her own lord do this to her? Looking over at Ka-bal Lavina said "Why did you do this?" in a faint whisper "Why you ask? This is the event that will set the beginning of the end... Your death will bring the chosen one to me, and I will have complete rule over all Zephyr. Plus it's enjoyable to watch you suffer" he began to laugh a wicked and treacherous laugh. Although he did not know who the chosen one was for certain, he knew she would have a role in his findings.

Lavina's torso started to float around the room for a while until Nexius said "IT IS DONE THE TWO WILL BECOME ONE!!!" Her body flew across the room as if she was a rag doll hitting the wall exploding. Ka-bal got up and clapped his hands together as if it was the best form of entertainment he had ever saw, her lifeless body was amusement to him. Her soul exited her corpse and she stood to her feet "am I...?" Ka-bal completed her sentence and said "dead, yes your dead and I am going to fulfill my promise you will be with Vertic for all eternity" she looked back at the vortex of swirling blue and black colors that circulated from the floor. Shadows arouse from it and grabbed her taking her slowly towards the pit. Lavina fought and struggled to get lose from the tight grasps of the shadows but every attempt was unsuccessful. Ka-bal got up and told Nexus, "If you ever decide to leave, this would be your fate as well!" Nexius held his head low and did not reply. He was in shame that he was apart of all this and allowed Ka-bal to use his magic for murder and deception.

Chapter 2

King Ka-bal was not born into royalty contrary to his demeanor that he was higher than the gods; he was abandoned when he was just a baby and was found in a bunch of bushes. He was wrapped in the finest of clothes in front of the royal kingdom. Nobody knew where he came from not even King Arion's servants the ones that found him. When presented to King Arion in his royal champers, he instantly fell in love with this baby not even caring where he came from.

He named him Ka-bal because the clothe he was wrapped in was made from the most prestigious of places called the "Ka-balizin nectar" which only the royal families in the world wore. From then on, Ka-bal became part of the royal family and future heir of the throne. Through the years Arion raised Ka-bal to be selfless and compassionate to others, but even a father knows what their son is capable of and he watched him over the years growing more and more unconscious of the affairs of the kingdom and more self-absorbed and mean. He didn't behave like a normal Zephyrian would nor looked much like one either. Ka bal was very tall and very wide but in a good way. He always wore shiny gold thick armor that stared from his shoulders down to his fee and gantlets on both hands. He is very good lookings with a scar that ran across his face from his right temple to his left check but that didn't stop the ladies from being all over him, not just because he was King but because he was striking. He was a beige in color which was very unusual. His hair was spikey like a fiery flame which made him more appealable.

A Zephyrian's life span is about 1000 years and as they grow older they developed white stripes on their necks which reveal how old they are. For every 50 years we develop a white stripe on our neck and it continues to grow upward until we die. We had distinctive faces, our two ears on each side with many piercing were long and curved downward at the tip. Our skin was a deep red varying between male and female. Usually males were considerably darker then the females. Usually we all wore our hair long and tied back with decorative beads and feathers in them.

King Arion was one of the greatest kings that ever lived. He passed down his thrown 189 years before he died of natural causes because his adopted son Ka-bal insisted that he needed to stand down. King Arion was a gentle man but he was no push over, but with Ka-bal he let him get his way quite often. Ka-bal was manipulative and the embodiment of the purest form of evil, he pretended to love and care but he really only thought of how he could desecrate others.

Before Ka-bal sentenced Vertic to his death in the Arena he devised a plan to keep Vertic as his leading knight due to Vertic wanting to leave and marry Lavina. In other words, there was never a way out if you served Ka-bal you served him till death either in the battle field or through his own "entertainment" as he called it. "Verdic, my one true friend will you join me in a feast to commemorate all you have done for me and Bawurr". Verdic did not hesitate; he loved Ka-bal and trusted him with all of his heart and soul. "Yes I will my lord it would be my honor" Ka-bal quickly gathered all his servants to prepare a festive celebration. Vertic thought this celebration was because he was finally going to retire from his duty as Ka-bals lead Knight, little did he know Ka-bal never lets anyone go even if they did their time by his side.

Ka-bal said to Verdic "The time you spent by my side has not been unnoticed. You are ready to settle down with Miss Lavina and raise a family." Vertic stopped and held his breath for a moment; he was enthused that his King was letting him go. "Yes your greatness, I love her past the moon and the stars, when I see her I don't see any other her love is the only love that sustains me, when I feel her time stands still and when I kiss her death could take me and my heart would still be intertwined with hers"

Ka-bal was sickened by the amount of affection he saw, he only heard one thing out of Vertics mouth and that was "death could take me". He paused for a moment and drank from his large royal glass and said "I'll give you one chance to leave your duties in my army so you can be with Lavina for the rest of your lives". Verdict repeated "One chance? What do you mean" "Oh yes one chance" said Ka-bal. "You will face the Agantus tomorrow and if victory is yours, you will be released from your royal duties and will be freed from my army"

Vertic's heart shattered as if it was made of glass and it was knocked off a counter to break in a million pieces. All he could think of was how Lavina would react if he was to tell her that he could only be with her if he fought the greatest beast that as of now has been un-defeated. Vertic walked away from Ka-bal and didn't touch his dinner, he had too much anxiety not because he was afraid of losing against Agantus but for losing Lavina forever if he could not be victorious.

As the leader of Ka-bals army, Vertic led Bawurr in many victories. He fought successfully in the Sarianas wars. Vertic was 312 years old and joined the army at the age of 197. In relation to the lower life forms such as earth every 100 years for us is only 10 years on earth. The Sarianas wars lasted 100 years which was the shortest wars in Ka-bals reign. Ka-bal wanted his kingdom to be feared and demanded that every surrounding kingdom submit to him. There were 6 major cities in all of Zephyr which were Murdrik, Sarianas, Tanali, Raka, Aknoli and Bawurr. The rest of the world consisted of beautiful wild life, flowing rivers, mountains and vast oceans.

Zephyr cloaked itself by magic so it would be unseen from other surrounding planets. By day it has hovered by three orange suns and by night three gray moons. Magic sustained the planet and kept the city thriving. Every building was imbued with the elemental powers which came in handy if there ever was a war the cities rebuild i self with little assistance. The buildings were tall and ran high almost to the sky floating in air detached from each other. Every city was unique and had its own design. Bawurr was the most advanced and largest of all the cities.

Out of all the cities, the city of Sarianas was a city of peace. King Javos made sure his people were taken care of that's why his people loved him. Ka-bal sent a messenger to Javos and asked him for a sit down meeting. Before this, Sarianas and Bawurr had neither little communication between each other nor any conflict in King Arions rule. When King Ka-bal arrived at Sarianas he met Javos in his castle. "Welcome friend, we have been waiting for your arrival I assume your travels were peaceful" Javos said, Ka-bal had a grin on his face and shook his hand. "Yes Javos it was fine, I am grateful for your time and for meeting with me"

Javos was a dwarf very short in stature he had a large head with not one hair on his body. He wore green and white garments which were the most expensive and prestigious that fit his royalty. His crown was titled to the side as if he was an undeveloped child trying to wear a crown that did not fit him well. He was just a small King but none the less a great one.
Javos's servants set up a table of the finest foods and wine. He sat in a high chair with a booster as if he was an infant. Ka- bal did not look at his food his objective was to tell Javo that he wanted to take his kingdom

from him. Javos wife Ophine and son Menahi were sitting in between the large decretive table.

Ophine was very pretty, in fact gorgeous and had many jewels and diamonds around her neck and hands even down to her ankles reflected her royalty. When she walked every one stopped and appreciated her beauty. Menahi was a young Zephyrian, he was only 79 the earthly age equivalence of 8 or 9. He resembled much of Javo having no hair and big eyes that were the bluest you ever seen. He was not a dwarf and took after his mother in that aspect with his good looks and charm. He admired his father and for such a young Zephyrian he studied his father and all the books about what he had accomplished wanting to be just like him.

"So my friend what brings you here in such urgency?" Javos said Ka- bal got straight to the point and said "Your kingdom is weak and needs Bawurr to rule them. Javos was thrown aback from the blunt statement that proceeded out of Ka- bal's mouth. "What you ask is obscured!" Javos slammed his hand to the table causing his cup filled with expensive wine to fall over. One cup of wine would cost 1000 Zylos which was enough to feed a whole family for a whole year. Ophine shouted "you come to our city and demand such a repulsive thing from us? You can go back to your city the answer is no!"

Ka- bal got out of his seat and walked over to Javos. Javos held his knife in his hand clenching it with a forceful grip. Ka-bal asked him with a sly grin on his face "is that your final answer?" Javos replied with fury and impatience "G-E-T...O-U-T!" Ka-bal was pleased with his response and grabbed the back of Javos head and slammed his face into the knife he was holding piercing both his right eye and Ka-bals hand. Javos body shook with much compulsion until he quickly stopped moving. His wife screamed and ran towards Ka-bal to get him off Javos. Ka-bal took his Hand off the knife that cut threw his hand as well and it began to re generate itself in seconds.
"Ahhhhhhhhhhh!!!!" she screamed "You Bastard!"

Ophine took a swing at Ka-bal but he telekinetically pushed her in the air onto the floor. He picked her body up into thin air ripping off her flesh leaving nothing; only her blood and bones were exposed. Screaming with such great anguish He moved his hands weaving them around and threw an orb like bolt hitting her body and causing her to semi explode then implode until every bones in her body was diminished. Her jewels flew out on to the floor with her blood as their signature.

Menahi's heart fluttered it was jumping out of his chest, he fell to the ground off his chair and slid across the room to the nearest wall "Moooommmmmm!!!" he squealed barely getting the words out. The two guards in the room ran towards Ka-bal pulling out their swords, Ka-bal grabbed Javos by his clothes and dished him out the window. He threw a smoke bomb that engulfed the room and clouded him as he made his escape out the window as well. Ka-bal landed on the hard grassy floor making indents with his feet, he ran with Javos body towards the Isona fields just outside the gates of Sarianas.

When Ka-bal reached Bawurr he put Javos head on a large pole outside the city to exploit his victory. Menahi though young and inexperienced became King of Sarianas and vowed to seek revenge for his parents. Pulsaire was Menahi's mentor in the king-ship; he faithfully taught him how to rule at an early age as well as being a friend helping him recover from his disturbing loss of his parents. Menahi was still grieving he had a responsibility that only he could fulfill, years had passed but Menahi was still going to make Ka-bal pay for what he did to his family.

Menahi angrily sent his army to Bawurr even though Pulsaire recommended he didn't. When his troops got to Bawurr they were met by Agantus who devoured all of his troops not leaving one alive. This endless bloodshed and feud continued for the next 100 years. Back and forth both Bawurr and Sarianas until one day

Menahi was 179 years of age, decided to catch Bawurr by surprise. Menahi did not go by only land but went to the skies for help, he conjured up 270 of the Casaronti which were strong winged creatures made by the element of thunder and lighting and crashed down on Bawurr destroying buildings and killing many innocent lives.

For hours the city was in chaos and ruins with screaming and yelling for Ka-bal to make his move. Ka-bal then gathered his greatest of mages from Nexius Tower and his army and made steadfast movement to the Isona fields. In the final battle there were 20,000 troops in all from Bawurr and 16,700 troops from Sarianas. The slaying went on for days as with no sleep or rest until the battle was done.

For three days they fought a horrific blood shed of a fight, Ka-bal ordered his mages to resurrect the fallen corps and filled them with a temporary magic of life that made them like soulless zombies until their roles of defeating the Sarianas was in completion. The armies both attacked with swords and bows slaying endlessly with a countless amounts of bodies, Ka-bal decided to end it all when he ran in their gates running up to were Menahi throne was.

"I have waited 100 years for this! You killed both my parents leaving me in this world alone... My hate for you transcends beyond anything known to any Zephyrian and I will be the one to kill and over throw you!!!" Ka-bal laughed a wicked laugh that echoed through the halls "let us finish this... I left you alive for this moment of hate and rage... I killed your parents for my own amusement, now I will end you".

Menahi took his daggers and lunged at Ka-bal stabbing in his chest and stomach Ka-bal fell down in a fetal position as if he was defeated. Menahi kicked his face so hard he back flipped into the air breaking the hard wooden table, the same table that they ate at before Ka-bal slaughtered his family. Menahi shot magic unto the ceiling causing it to fall on Ka-bal, the thick stone and rock fell on Ka-bal with a major impact causing his body to be still. Menahi vengeance was complete; he'd finally defeated his parent's betrayer and murderer.

Menahi was feeling a strange sensation and found it hard to breathe as if his breath was being robbed from his very essence. He flew back above his thrown seat and his arms and legs were spread as if he was pinned against the wall. Ka-bal regained his composure and got up from the debris that was on him, he threw Menahi's dagger into his stomach and it began to spiral rapidly into his intestine. Menahi gasp struggling to get air as he felt the blade twist and move further into him, "Father...... Mother..... Sarianas.... I have failed you all" he said with his final words. Ka-bal pushed his almost lifeless body into the solid wall, smashing his body into the rocks and the blood began to pour out of his skin until he was a part of the wall. Ka-bal raised both his hands, Menahi's body slowly started to become stone embedded into the wall above his throne. That was his mark and that was his statement that he would be a force to be reckoned with. Now Menahi would live his life as a statue overlooking the memories where his parents were slain.

Ka-bal left the castle, the war was done and Vertic and 568 troops out of 20,000 were left standing. Vertic was uninjured despite the constant classing of swords and piercing arrows thrown at him. From that day forth Ka-bal promoted him to become his leading knight "I accept my lord" Vertics ignorance and unwise acceptance would later lead to his death.

Chapter 3

When I heard the news that Lavina was dead I
was in a state of disbelief. I was angry and filled with

immeasurable amount of deteriorating pain. She was my sister and I loved her and now she is gone. I could handle her passing with ease because I know she went to Isara without a shadow of a doubt, but I could not accept that she was murdered so maliciously. My world ended at that very moment! I was going to kill her murderer and redeem Lavina!

Ka- bal approached me, he knew me by name. "Reaven I send my deepest condolences to you. I know you have had a lot of lost in your life and this just adds to your pain. If there is anything the Royal family could do please there is nothing to great or to much that would be enough." I had no words my mouth went dry as if I had not eat or drank anything in 40 days and 40 nights. "I want the head of my sister's killer. I want him to have the same fate; I'll send him to the Gregorie in pieces!!!" Ka-bal hesitated as if Reaven's eyes saw right through him "We will find your sisters killer and justice will be served, I swear it."

Reaven's eyes filled with water and he started to breathe heavily. "Such rage and passion" Ka-bal said "I could use that in my Army" Reaven said in such a deep dark voice replied "I will serve you and I will find my sisters killer." "You will find her killer. I am sure of it" Ka-bal reached out his hand and touched Reavens shoulder and said "it's time to prepare you. I am confident you will be a great warrior just as your father was" "You knew my father?" "Of course I did he a good friend and a good soldier"

I grew up in the inner city of Bawurr we were the lower class and not many Zephyrians associated them-self with us because of our status. Lavina and I were close, our parents died in battle against the Murdrik when i was only 150 years old which in earthly time it would equate to a child that was about 11 or 12 considering our life span is estimated to around 1000 years. Lavina was 106 years older than I was and she was able to look after me in the absents of my parents. When she met Vertic he was a young knight and recently joined Ka-bals army.

Lavina was walking in the market place and was attacked by a Kepler, they are ugly creatures who take what they want and if that involved taken a life they will do so. Keplers had four arms and two legs with decent sized claws that helped them become very agile and fast. Their skins was slimy and smooth which made it hard to confine them if you had the privilege of capturing one, they had 3 tails that they used as a lethal and deadly weapon. Their faces were short and had their tiny teeth were razor sharp. They had two large horns that came out of its temple that were used to pierce its victims also paralyzing them in the process.

As Lavina was walking she felt the hands of the Kepler grab her and threw her to the ground, she tried fighting back but he just kicked her against the wooden table that had fresh fruits and vegetables on it. The table broke and the produce scattered around the area, some locals grabbed them and ran with stolen goods. Most Zephyrians would walk by and mind their business in fear that the Kepler would get them as well. Vertic lashed out with his sword slicing the Keplers large horn the Kepler swung his long tail and Vertic dodged it, he then impaled his massive gold sword into the Kepler impaling its stomach it let out a loud yell then the creature fled.

The rest of the guards ran after the Kepler throwing binding matter at its feet compelling it to the ground. The guards pressed their swords against its neck decapitating it neck from its body and killing it. Lavina was wounded; she had a large scratch on her forehead that was bleeding as well as a hurt ankle. Vertic helped her up and cleaned her wound. "You're okay now" Vertic looked at her with passion and desire and she felt it because she looked at him the same way. From that moment on they were inseparable. They quickly fell in love as if it was destined that a sudden face of death the two would find love and happiness in an unfortunate circumstance.

For eons, Zephyrians have passed down a story of a Savior that would rise from the dead and reclaim peace and order to the land from an evil tyrant. This messiah was to bring balance not only for the living but for the lost souls that needed retribution. There were two places that a soul would go after their life on Zephyr was over either Isara or Gregorie. Isara was a blissful paradise, nowhere in Zephyr was like it. Tales of Isara and its beauty and peace was passed down from generation to generation. Only there would a Zephyrian would ever truly find rest and peace. But for every paradise there is a tormented place, a place where there was no rest and you relive your death repetitively over and over and over. Gregorie was a place of exile, it contained many foul beasts that took innocent lives and caused chaos throughout their life time.

Those tales just seemed like stories to me growing up, I did not care about myths, I just wanted Lavina and Vertic back! I prepared myself for Lavinas and Vertics ceremony. I stood still and tall as if I was paralyzed. I felt that if i stood still long enough that time would stop and this would all be a terrible dream that I was waiting anxiously to wake up from. For a Zephyrian, we didn't bury our dead we put them on a magical talus and covered them as if they were a sleep. The talus was transparent and floated in air up to the skies.

They hovered over the ocean and ascended upward in hopes that the Zephyrian would reach Isara.

As I watched the knights take the two bodies, I felt a great pain in my chest it was as if someone reached into my chest and was squeezing my heart clenching it without any remorse. I hated this, I was angry and all I could think of was revenge. I walked up to Lavina's corps and grabbed her hand. "I will make them pay for what they did to you. Whoever they are I will not sleep until I find your murderer" tears ran down my face as I let her hand go, I walked away in despair.

Ka-bal started to make a speech to the crowd "These are the fallen from our kingdom and their deaths will not be in vain. They were one of us and will live on in Isara" His heart felt speech seemed genuine and true. Tesious approached me and said she was sorry for my loss. I have not seen Tesious in over 130 years since Ka-bal took her from being a servant to his Queen. We grew up together in Bawurr and we were best friends, as we grew older we developed feelings for each other but never truly expressed it to one another.

Tesious had a facial expression I have never seen as if she was guilty of something, I didn't know why she looked this way but I just thought she was saddened by all that deaths that transpired. Tesious kissed my cheek and told me that she always loved me and she wished things were different I hugged her and said "you will always be my love but your hand belongs with Ka-bal" as we ended the intimate huge, King Ka-bal entered and saw us. He said "Are you alright Reaven?" he had a suspicious look on his face as if he knew that there was more to this hug. I replied "Yes my lord as long as you are well I am well"

"You need some rest Reaven" Ka-bal said "Go to the 6th floor there you will have a bed and the servants will please you" Reaven departed from Tesious and said "Thanks my lord" he left Tesious and went to the 6th floor to his room. There he was greeted by the most exotic Zephyrians who gave me great pleasure and comfort.

Chapter 4

Now that I was a knight in the army my feelings for Tesious could never surface. I loved her and that would never change, but she was married to Ka-bal. I served under Ka-bal for over 200 years and every victory we accomplished it brought me a little more satisfaction for what happened to Vertic and Lavina. Sarianas was already taken in the Sarianas wars and Javos head was still posted in front of the gates of Bawurr. Ka-bal was adamant about taken over all the major cities and justified it with the rationale that he would be a better fit of being king of all of Zephyr. At the time I believed it as well and helped him take over Tanali, Raka, Aknoli and Murdik. Countless of bodies fell before our blades eventually the other cities such as Tanali and Raka just handed their thrones to us without any questioning. The whole world was in Ka-bals hands and he was now more than just a king, he was like a god. Over the years Ka-bal became less emotionless and more of a tyrant, he executed anyone who did not agree with what he said or tortured them for days, sometimes both.

Nevertheless I still followed him no matter what kind of King he was. A foolish mistake I would soon discover was a bad mistake. One day, Ka-bal took me to the side and asked me to come to dinner with him. I was pleased with this purposal considering no one ever eats with the king besides his wife Tesious. "Yes my lord it would be my honor." "Go get washed up and changed, I have prepared a feast for us." I was unsure what it was about, but anything like this from the king was always a good thing.

When I arrived at the dining room, the table was set up for royalty. Ka-bal said "Please sit my friend" I sat at the chair opposite from him which was quite a distance considering the size of the room . I indulged myself with the beautiful selection of assorted foods and drank the finest of wines. After we were done Ka-bal said to me "Reaven you have been with me for over 200 years and your hard work and dedication has paid off. I am offering you a higher position as my lead knight" I looked at him with a blank expression, "My lord that is a great honor one I am not sure I can fulfill." "Vertic was with me he contributed so much to me and this kingdom and I see the same attributes in you" "Thank you my lord, I'll do my best to please you" Ka-bal smiled and was pleased of my acceptance.

The next morning I opened my eyes and got dressed. I haven't slept like that since Lavina had died. I left the room that the king let me rest in and went into the dining area once again. There was a huge table that had so much food it could feed the whole streets of Bawurr. I did not understand why they went hungry when the palace had all this food; everyday Ka-bal had large quantities of food for breakfast, lunch and dinner. "Reaven please sit and eat with me my friend" I sat down feeling uneasy considering this is the second day in a row he has been so kind to let me eat in his presence "Today you will go see the Osawa, they will lead you to the right direction. Do not be nervous, for they speak the truth and know all"

Ka-bal grinned and said "you will meet the Osawa and they will tell you your destiny". Before anyone was initiated in the army they are to go to the Osawa and sought out their wisdom so they would understand their purpose. I never felt that I had any purpose but to be a blacksmith for Barkiss who gave me my first job. Barkiss was my father's friend and took me under his mentorship when I was younger; I always looked up to him and admired him. He died alongside my parents leaving Lavina and I alone.

Once we were done eating we got on the Yenin to get to our destination by air. The Yenin are massive birds that were used as a way of transportation. The Yenins two wings overlapped each other spreading out far and wide. They walked on their hands and feet because their spines were developed that way. Their faces were green and they have small mouths with many little teeth. Their sides had long black tentacles that soldiers often used in battle to hang from and charge right into battle.

The Yenin flapped its wings and in one blow we were elevated to the sky. I looked over the city of Bawurr in amazement I had never seen Zephyr from this angle. The whole world I was on top of and saw everything from the great lakes and rivers to all of the surrounding cities i was in awe. The Yenin flew gracefully; soaring through the clouds then descending between the mountains of Keltz. "You never done this before Reaven" King Ka-bal said. "Never my lord this is truly amazing" I replied. "Well this won't be the last you and I are going to do great things for Bawurr and the rest of Zephyr!" I tried focusing on both the scenery and Ka-bal but it was all too overwhelming.

We flew for several hours to the far North to the forest of Pierce Kod. Pierce Kod was an island that was secluded from civilization; it was filled with the most unusual vegetation and wild life. Ka-bal jumped off the Yenin, "Come on the doors are up ahead" I got off and walked with him. "Sir there are no doors" Ka-bal reached for his Royal crest and repeated the words "Inox Arburum" the rocks began to slide into each other creating an entrance so we can proceed. I walked in this enormous monument and could not believe the wonders of this place, it was a cave hidden within a large mountain. No one would ever have thought this place was a secret cave and the wonders that it had inside.

We continued to walk and images of my life appeared on the walls. The images looked like I was seeing a reflection in water. Every few steps i took a new image appeared. I saw the time when I was young with my parents and we were all a real family before they died. The walls reflected my thoughts and my emotions they knew more about me then I knew about myself. I paused for a second, "what's wrong?" Ka-bal said I ignored his words because my focus was on what I saw next.

I saw a depiction of Lavina and the last time we were together. I remember that as if it just happened, "She told me she was finally starting a life with Verdic and that she was pregnant with his seed" It took everything in me not to let the tears fall down my eyes. I walked away hoping no one saw what just happened. "Only you can see what the walls reveal" Ka-bal said, I was relieved that my personal memories stayed my own.

After a long peregrination that seemed ceaseless, we reached our destination at the end of the cave, there was nothing wondrous to see... no mystical creatures... no great prophet... no mage with great power... Nothing!!! King Ka-bal spoke into the empty large room "OSAWA! I come before you so you can share your secrets with me" we waited and nothing seemed to have happened. "Osawa! It is I the King of

Bawurr please show yourself!!!" The Cave shook and strange images showed them self as if we were in a hologram of some sort. Out of nowhere three eyes opened that were on the walls this miraculous cave was not only beautiful but it was ALIVE!

The Osawa was not a person or a mystic but it was three set of eyes that circled the room. Each eye had a different shape and color to it. The first eye had a flame as its pupil the second was blue like water and ice and the third eye was very distinctive green that looked like nature. It did not have a mouth to speak from nor ears to hear but it just gazed at us with a piercing look as if it was analyzing your soul.

The Osawa looked at Ka-bal and said "Ka-bal you have already been forewarned that you are the damnation of this world. Even after you are gone, generations are still going to be plagued by your tyrant rule. You will bring death and chaos to this world and others... You have no place here" I did not understand what the Osawa was trying to say, up until now I thought Ka-bal was a great king and had no flaws. I thought to myself, why would these creatures say such horrific things about my king? "I would watch your tongue if I was you creature you are talking to the King!" Ka-bal faced me and said "It is okay. There words are not without purpose" I was perplexed Ka-bal would allow it but I kept my opinion to myself.

Ka-bal said to the Osawa "I know my purpose! I know what I will do but I came here for him! IS HE THE ONE!?" The Osawa's eyes glanced in my direction they circled around me for a moment. I looked at the walls of the cave and saw ruins and darkness of the once great city of Bawurr. The eye's surrounded me and said

"Reaven....

I call you by name...

You are the one...

You are not who you think you are...

Your parents bore you but did not create you...

They nurtured you but did not conceive you...

You are the divine....

You are the god of the Zephyrians....

Now it's time to fulfill your destiny and release the souls that are trapped in Gregorie....

Betrayed by whom you serve...

It is through your pain others shall live, and through your death you shall rise....

Your death is what Legends are made of....

"YOU'RE SUFFERING.... S-H-A--L-L... B-E... L-E-G-E-N-D-A-R-Y!!!.........."

Ka-bal was infuriated he grabbed me by my neck ignoring the Osawa and with one powerful blow, one punch that sent me straight to the ceiling of the cave, on my way back down he kicked me and upon impact my chest caved in as I hit the hard cold rocks. I heard my arms and legs snap I had never felt anything break before, in fact I have never felt pain like this up until now. I have fought many battles and some of the toughest creatures that have inhabited the land of Zephyr, but fighting Ka-bal was different. I blacked out immediately and was unconscious for several hours.

Chapter 5

Ka-bal ordered his guards to take me to Nexius tower which was located on the highest floor in a separate part building next to the castle. Ka- bal commanded Nexius to open the Door of Akrium, I have heard the name before, my father told me stories about the Door of Akrium it was a conduit between the world of the living and the world of spirits. Up until now it has only been a story as that my father has told me but everything that he had told me as a child has inexorably been fulfilled.

Nexius began to chant words that were unknown even to me. I have heard my mother recite magic but never to this magnitude, had he begun to recite these words "O-D-A-Y........ N-A-S-A-Y COME IN TO ME O-D-A-Y... N-A-S-A-Y COME IN TO ME" his eyes turned white and his hair were substituted by white and blue flames so bright it was blinding. His body began to levitate upward and wind circulated around him as if he was in the eye of a terrible storm.

His chanting grew louder, even without pupil's his stare was inescapable and frightful. His arms turned into water and his body was that of the element of the ground. He had morphed into the elements of life. Consequently, for me it meant death, I knew I was dying I could not feel anything. The only thing that made me know that I was amongst the living was that my peripheral vision was still intact and was able to barley see my surroundings, only hearing Nexius chant as he proceeded with his ritual. A Black like vortex formed from the floor and my body as dismantled as it is was being pulled towards it. The agony was overbearing and my demise was to come shortly after. Ka-bal was anxious to end my life and I was in awe why he was doing this to me, someone who was as loyal and dedicated to him. Nexius was in control of my body I was at his disposal, I did not recognize this altitude of affliction but I did find comfort in Ka-bal's immanent vexation. I was still alive.... surviving longer than most would have.... I was not dead yet... but I knew it not be for long...

"My lord... why are you doing this to me? have I not served you all this time?" Ka-bal replied with an agitated tone "You foolish little boy... Have you not put the pieces together? I have used you all this time... I was the one who killed your family both mother and father... I even set up arrangements for Vertic and Lavina to be placed in Gregorie! Isara is far from where they are they are all where I want them to be!" "WHAT!? What are you saying? You killed them?" "Yes! I even purposely married Tesious the one you loved all this time! You think I didn't know? I purposely took away everyone and everything you loved one by one!!!" "But why??? WHY DID YOU DO THIS TO ME! YOU TOOK MY LIFE AWAY!!! I HAVE DONE NOTHING BUT TRY AND PLEASE YOU MY WHOLE LIFE!!!" Ka-bal laughed a dark and wicked laughter, "That's the irony of it all, you were supposed to be Zephyr's savior but now you will die never being able to fulfill any of it" "You piece of shit!!! I promise I will kill you and make you suffer a hundred times more then what you did to them!!!" "Well that will be kind of hard to do considering in a few moments you will be dead... Think of it like this, you will be reunited with your family" Ka- bal laughed as he walked away with his back towards me, that just angered me even more. He stepped to the side of the room, I hated myself for being his pawn all these years but at this point there was nothing I could do.

Nexius was at the peak of his capacity, his strength of magic surge through him as if he was the creator of the whole universe, I had felt nothing like this in my 356 years of living he was going to end me by the greatest of magic banishing me into an eternity of Gregorie. Questions circulated through my mind why did he do this? Why did Ka-bal's demeanor change so drastically? Why was my family involved? I was bewildered, Nexius was ready to focus his magic that he started and was not going to stop until his work was completed. He was ready, fully prepared for what extracting my soul into Gregorie.

Indescribable pain as I felt my rib cage rip in desolate places outside my chest. My bones were crushed and turned in every direction imaginable with no plea loud enough to make it end. Time seemed to stand still as I attempted to scream but eventually my vocal cords ripped apart until i was choking on my own blood. The torment for any Zephyrian would normally last a few moments, but this punishment was Ka-bal's edict to the citizens of Zephyr that his sovereignty would not be defiled. Anguish seeped through my flesh through every body part, even the tips of my hairs screamed to exude this treacherous brutishness that caused my lost tranquility. Ka-bal ensured that I would suffer the greatest demise that was ever bestowed upon on a Zephyrian.

Seconds turning into Minutes, minutes turning into hours, hours seemed like an eternity... It was true, the Osawa was right... I was the one that would be betrayed and sentence to damnation, despite me being his most loyalist and most dedicated servient. Ka-bal made sure I would endure the harshest sentence. Was this for loving Tesious? What did he mean when he said that I was the savior? I was confused... lost in my own transgressions.

Flashes of my life appeared before my eyes just like I saw it in the walls of the cave of the Osawa. I saw Lavina.... My Parents... Vertic... Tesious ... My hatred for Ka-bal was un-containable it poured out of me like a volcanic eruption... I couldn't die like this, who would avenge their deaths as well as my own? I was defeated and hopeless, it didn't hurt too much now I was becoming numb all over.

In the final moment before my passing from this world to the next, the words of the Osawa appeared to me and suddenly my pain was over "Your suffering will be legendary" What did they mean? Was I truly a god of this world? Was my family really not my own?

Time cease to exist and my pain was no more.... This is where my legacy begins. .

Chapter 6

I felt my self-fading; my soul was exiting the realm of the living and entering a new dimension. I descended down a long tunnel of colors and swirls my eyes were in amazement. Where was I headed? I was moving at a rapid yet slow and steady pace downward, I felt as if i was gliding to a place where I can finally find rest. The beautiful swirls of complex colors formulated swirls of burning flames that swirled around me. I was afraid I started falling faster and faster without any walls or ledges to grab on to. The flames were getting hotter and burning my skin, parts of my body were burnt off exposing bone, muscle and tissue.

I saw the ends of the tunnel, what followed was fire and darkness. After I got through the tunnel of flaming fire I came rushing out of it, I began to fall into an open space down from great heights. I couldn't see much because the place was covered in smoke and mist that made it hard for me to see through. I collided into hard rocks, breaking most of my bones and hearing them snap out of place. There's no way I survived such impact I lost consciousness for what seemed like forever. I woke up to the crackling of my bones, they re-attached them-self getting back into place my skin healed almost instantly. "How is this possible" I asked myself. I got up and composed myself probing my surroundings still adjusting to my regeneration.

Listening closely I heard squealing of wild beasts. I looked up and saw a black disturbing looking creature. It flew around me like a predator searching for its prey, they drew closer and closer then flew directly towards me I quickly jumped out its way. This thing was flying without any wings! "What are you beast!?" I yelled "I am... What I am... we have been waiting for you... R--E--A--V--E--N"

"How do you know my name? Speak beast before I cut out your tongue and feed it to the scavengers" I said sharply. "F-o-o-l-i-S-H- b-O-Y-... Y-o-u-r in G-r-e-g-o-r-i-e... D-e-a-t-h has no p-o-w-e-r... h-e-r-e.... for we have never been of the l-i-v-i-n-g... my name is Strovos..." Strovos was gray in color his face was half bones with bits of flesh on him. He had one eye and the other one had warms that came out of it. His hands were long, sharp and bloody as if he just used them to claw something to death. There was something crawling around in his hollow eye socket, a small snake like figure. It came out his eye but it was attached to his skull somehow and said "I am Faeus. We have been waiting for your return"

"Return? How could I return to a place I've never been?" I was angry and confused the events that were happening were so fast I could not grasp any understanding. First I died then I am in Gregorie... "I do not understand!" Faeus and Strovos acted very strangely they talked to each other frequently ignoring me as if I wasn't even there, I guess the absence of others and chronic seclusion forced them to become introverted. Strovos who spoke slow and sounded as if he was out of breath, he looked at Faeus and said "H-e does n-o-t R-E-M-E-B-E-R...W-h-a-t... t-o... d-o... " Faeus said to Strovos and this time including myself in the conversation "Let us show you the foreign" Strovos completed Faeus's sentence "F-o-l-l-o-W - u-s W-E make you r-e-m-e-m-b-e-r...."

Strovos and Faeus dashed into the air and headed towards a cliff. I ran but could not keep up with them "Hey!!! I do walk to get around you know" as I got to the end of the cliff I heard faint sounds of agony. As I came upon the cliff I lost my focus and the rocks beneath me fell apart, I fell hitting just about every rock, bolder, and stone on my way down. I got up and Strovos and Faeus were very still with a blank expression on their face pointing at the source of the strange noises and which direction they were coming from.

My un-beating heart felt like it was being ripped out my chest. I never realize how alive I was until all of my organs were no longer functioning. I saw decrepit Zephyrians who walked aimlessly like zombies. Some crawling on the floor eating their own hands! Others in chains crying to be released and in torment! The screams were horrific! I had to accept that Gregorie was my home now, I was sent here due to my king's betrayal. .

Strovos and Faeus began to poke fun at the fallen Zephyrians saying "We call them the bile of Gregorie... They are just waste" the two began to laugh inappropriately I instantly grabbed Faeus yanking him by his slimy neck Strovos lifted his hand spreading his long pointy fingers out, shadow like vines came from the ground and wrapped around my throat. The other two held my arms, legs and torso almost creating a chair to hold me in place.
I could not move even if I tried, "You think this is funny to watch my Zephyrian brothers and sisters suffer!" Faeus replied "They are NOT yours... You never were or ever will be a Zephyrian" "If I am not a Zephyrian then what or who am I?" Faeus said "You are Ka-bals counterpart, Ka-bal was created by Gregorie and you from Isara. The Essence of Fates formed the two of you so there would be equalibrum in Zephyr. You are brothers on opposing sides trying to fulfill the balance of life."

In my mind I refused to believe it... My heart no matter how dead it was knew they were telling the truth but why would they help me if I was to restore Isara? "Why do you help me? Why don't you just kill me" Strovos and Faeus both laughed "It would be hard to kill what is already dead, we may be enemies but there still needs to be a balance. All of us need to move faster, time has no influence here but time still continues on Zephyr! I'll take you to The Essence of Fates for they will tell you how to get back the world of the living..."

"What could they possibly do for me now?" I sharply asked "I am dead there is nothing anyone can do for me" You are the one that rises from the Gregorie, your death was only the beginning" Faeus went back in Strovos eye. Strovos showed me the rest of Gregorie, it was too much for my stomach to handle. Gregorie was an unsettling place; it was an endless tomb of rocks, cliffs, fire, burning flesh, cries and pain. We moved past the rocks to see a city of imprisonment, there were beast of all stature walking around feeding off the flesh of former Zephyrians.

Fire burned their skins melting their indestructible bodies. They regenerated once someone was dead (again). There were tall sharp blades that impaled these Zephyrians screaming to get down. Walking through a grave yard of the forgotten was devastating, I could not do anything about it I was useless. Thoughts raced through my head, will I ever get out? Did Ka-bal send everyone that I loved down here? If he did he sent them here? Knowing this is what Ka-bal wanted for me to have regrets, to have hatred towards him and it was working. I'm going to find a way to get to him, I have to know why he did what he did, and I know my answer will be found sooner than later...

Chapter 7

Fate placed me in an inexorable cycle that could not be escaped. This place is the epitome of death and decay; I was forever trapped with no means of escape or the ability to avenge myself or my family. Stovos and Faeus showed me all the ways one could get tormented. It was grotesque, on the ground there was a severed hand on the floor moving towards an arm, the hand re-attached itself to the arm and moved towards a torso. I walked over to the body and collected the rest of the parts helping the corpse get back together. Then a large beast swung a large hammer descending downward at me, as I jumped back it hit the corpse and it exploded into many different pieces. Faeus yelled "You cannot interact with anyone!"

The fat beast with much girth had two heads covered with scales. It had eyes blinking from all around its body and other parts. Hands, legs, feet and arms were all throughout the creature. This savage consumed the bodies and they became a part of him! It smacked me with such force I flew back stumbling over the ground. Strovos quickly grabbed me and covered me in his cloak; the creature could not spot us for we blended into the darkness.

"If you ever want to get out of here you have to do exactly what we say! This world is not like Zephyr it is a place filled with very dangerous creatures! No matter what you do you cannot save them now... That time will come but not now." As we came closer to the prisons Strovos and Faeus announce their departure. "From here on you will have to go alone... Our place is not here but in the shadows of Gregorie" I asked "Well how will I know my way out of here?" They left without answering me leaving me utterly alone in darkness. Walking through the darkness and black mist was hard, I could not see a thing. After the mist disappeared I came across prison cells that many Zephyrians were confined in. Screams of horror echoed throughout the Caves, I notice a distinctive voice as I turned back I saw two bodies with no legs and their organs were being devoured by small creatures. Demons with four horns on their foreheads, they were scary looking with six eyes that were unusually small. Their jaws protruded outward with large sized fangs that looked like mini knifes.

I was drawn to the familiar voice and to my surprise I was taken aback; it was both Lavina and Vertic! "LAVINA!!!!!" I screamed, I kicked the little creatures off of them still remembering Faeus warned me not interact with anyone no matter what but I did not care that was my sister and I was going to save her!!! Lavina lifted her head and tears of joy and pain ran down her face, then she began to speak to me but her voice was scratchy from all the screaming she had done "Reaven... I'm so happy to see your but why are you here??? This place is not for you...." I told her to save her energy, "I am going to get you out of here" Vertic jumped in and said "we cannot leave out prison we were both sent here by Ka-bal and Nexius"

Suddenly the realization that Ka-bal was using me this whole time hit me hard and infuriated me, he took everything from me. "You have to go Reaven... I overheard the guards here say they are waiting for you... They call them self the Canthius... If they find you they will never let you fulfill your destiny as Isara's savior". "I can't let you stay down here any longer! I can't just walk away and leave you!" I said "You have to save Zephyr! Ka-bal only wants you to stay here because he knows your emotions will get the best of you. Please Reaven listen to me" Lavina jumped in and said.

Vertic screamed "Watch out!" The beast I encountered before grabbed me by my legs and my face smashed into the floor. He tossed my body out the room; I landed near the end of a cliff. As I looked down there was a pool of burning fire. Canthius charged at me and tackled me off the cliff. Falling down while Canthius attacking me with his claws. Strovos grabbed my hand saving me leaving the creature to bathe in the Fire pit. Strovos brought me back up and Faeus came out and said "If you want to save your sister and the rest of the world you can't get your self-trapped here forever!"

I lashed out saying "Why didn't you tell me she was here!!!" Faeus was angry he shouted "Because you can't save her now!!! You cannot take her back to the world of the living!!! Do you not understand? All this interaction with them will cause a disruption in the balance"
The ground began to shake and rocks started falling down, we were in the mists of an avalanche. Strovos took me in flight and we crossed the endless sea of fire once we got to the other side there were long steps leading into light. "Entering the light is forbidden for us dark dwellers. The Essence of fate is there" The quake began to shake harder, boulders falling from every direction smashing into other rocks causing explosions.

We caused a great disruption and the Canthius of all sizes multiplied in numbers trying to prevent me from leaving, "No one escapes Gregorie" They said. I quickly ran up the stairs dogging the falling rocks, the exit were slowly closing in so I moved as swiftly as I could. The beast was quick jumping on the walls and evading the falling debris, I knew I had to hurry. "You will never leave!!!" I kicked one of the beast stunning it long enough for a rock to smash its head into the steps, its brains leaked out from the sides of the rocks killing it instantly. There had to be 80 or even 100 more of them storming to not let me leave, Stovos yelled"R-u-N... l-n... T-o... t-H-e L-i-G-h-t" Feaus interceded saying "They cannot follow you there HURRY!!!"

The beast scratched my back while the radiance of the light covered the last few steps burning off its hand then causing its whole body to engulf in flames leaving nothing but ashes and a few bones. I jumped through the lighted doorway tumbling on the floor.

The darkness was over and I was in the world of spirits. The world of spirits could see the World of the living as if it was a one way mirror. Although I could see the world of the living this world was someone distorted and every object radiated with energy that misted off of it. Now I understood why many mystics often went to nature and claimed they were extracting power from nature. Everything has energy, everything is alive. Strovos and Faeus were not here to guide me any longer so I had to make it on my own to the Essence of Fate, Faeus had told me they could show me how to come back to the world of the living.... But how? I was dead I did not have a tangible body, nothing of substance; I was of no use in this form. I looked around this new environment and I was not surprised that I was in another tomb. The tomb was empty and hollow, no doors were present and I had no clue how to get out.

Whispers began faintly calling my name "R-e-a-v-e-n....R-e-a-v-e-n.....R-e-a-v-e-n....", they started to overlap each other in an echo. I felt like I was a pawn in a game and every move I made something else was dictating where I should go at every moment. My body started to become more transparent and I was unable to see, I was abruptly taken to an open field, it was a monumental wonder of paradise. The trees were tall and strong not tainted by construction or city life or even magic just pure bliss, I was in the Essence of fate. I explored the land observing the beautiful wild life and creatures some I have never seen before, even the insects were very distinctive and unusual.

I continued to hear the whispers; they were starting to get louder. I walked a straight path until I came across a huge tree "What do I do from here" I spoke to myself out loud. "Reaven..." a voice said "Who's there???" at this point I was use to so many surprises it began to be the norm. I walked up past the bushes and tall trees; it looked like paradise in seclusion. Waterfalls running from the mountain of rocks, in the center of the paradise were a small piece of land on it there was a gigantic chair made out of vines and leaves. Walking closer to it I noticed a white long beard that ran down to the ground its body was comprised of nature and branches and leaves.

"Savior...You do not know who you are just yet but all will be revealed to you. You were created to protect of all Zephyr" I hesitated to respond... "Who or what are you?" it picked itself up and hovered over me being taller than all of the other trees shooting up straight to the sky. "I am the fates. I will reveal your destiny but first you have to prove yourself worthy" I sharply replied "Worthy? I lost everything and my precious king condemned me to GREGORIE AND YOU TELL ME I HAVE TO PROVE MY SELF!" I said sarcastically.

The Tree of life sat down and gazed at me with a piercing look "You are not the first we have sent. The others have failed the trials and chose to use their hearts and did not fulfill their destiny... If you pass these test you will have your retribution" I got closer to the big pile of leaves and bark and said "What trials do you speak of?" The Tree of life responded "The first trial is the test of strength the second is the test of wisdom and the third is the test of compassion." I began to get agitated with being toyed with and said "You dare tell me I need to prove myself after all that has happened?" The Tree paused and the winds started storming all around me.

Water that was surrounding the Tree started coming up showing me images of those that had failed. "They wanted to forget, their creation came from both Isara and Gregorie. The balance of life is at constant war. Not even I have control over it but it must be stopped or Isara will be lost forever and Zephyr will be destroyed!" Prove that you're worthy Reaven, "If this is the way for me to kill Ka-bal I'll do it! He will pay for what he did to my family and to me!!!" "I warn you, don't let your emotions best you or you will wind up in Gregorie with the rest of the Canthius. They choose their fate and ignored their true destinies" "Are you saying that some of the Canthius were supposed to help with the balance between Isara and Gregorie?" "Yes, they failed and now serve an eternity making others suffer. If you fail you will suffer the same fate. Do you wish to proceed?" "Where others have failed I will succeed. I will free everyone from Gregorie."

The tree of life opened his vines and branches and created what seemed to be an opening of some sort. I hesitated looking into it was darkness; I walked towards its thick and complex assortment of leaves, vines, and roots. I slowly got closer to the door, the vines quickly closed behind me blocking the way back.

Chapter 8

I observed my surroundings and I was in a beautiful forest with the highest trees and the most peculiar animals. They were very distinctive all with black eyes without a soul or life within them. Just beings that exist without purpose nor meaning. All of these species here did not look like anything on Zephyr, they were bigger some with over grown teeth pointy ears large hands. There was something much different in this place than any other I have seen. I continued to walk through the forest and watch all these unusual creatures interact.

As I continued to walk I stepped into a pool of mucus that was green and yellow, it hardened causing my food to be unable to move. An overly sized bug that walked on 10 long legs jumped on top of my body forcing me to the ground without any weapons I was defenseless. It looked at me with its many eyes spitting out drool and disgusting mucus. It was going to eat me! I searched the ground for a rock or sharp stick but couldn't find anything. Then a four legged white and blue beast with large paws and a chattering mouth that I caught hiding in the bushes leaped out and used its claws to attack the over grown bug ripping at its body. They fought viciously until the four legged beast ripped off a piece of the bugs arm causing it to flee.

I finally was able to break the harden mucus off my feet and gained my composure. This forest paradise was revealing itself more of a deadly labyrinth, every time I turned around it seemed as if everything was changing, I was lost without any destination or knowing what I was looking for. "Ahhhh what am I doing here??? Where am I??? H-e-l-l-o any one here I am lost "I said out loud with a calm yet impatient voice. I heard a voice reply "You can't be lost if you don't know where you're going" I turned around and to my surprise there was an oasis filled with beautiful water that sparkled and waterfalls that were the bluest water I had ever seen. Once again the forest had changed.

Zephyr was beautiful but this was beyond what my eyes have ever experienced. Floating around was a Ball of light with something in the middle of it, it had no face or distinctive features it just flew around this glorious sanctuary as a shadow wrapped in light. "The names Detriku, and you I presume is Reaven" I took a step closer and replied "what is this place and how could you help me get back to the world of the living?" Detriku got closer to me and turned his shadowy body upside down getting close to my face and said "Straight to the point huh?" His voice was very child like it lacked any wisdom or knowledge so how could it be any use to me?

"You know it's very rude to think out loud!" Detriku said then started laughing "how did you....?" Before I got a word in he told me that he hears the thoughts of all spirits and feels them. "You are here because the tree of life wants you to discover your other, without your other you are pretty much dumb and useless" Detriku changed forms in front of my very eyes, as irritating as he was he was in the first 5 minutes I have been around him he was still fascinating. The light that covered him now became a shadowy radiance and his body became light. Steps appeared from the shadows and his body became an opening towards something, "If you want to save Zephyr you must obtain your other" I thought to myself what exactly is an other?

Detriku and his invasive mind reading loud mouth self said "It is your very being transcending to be a god. Every "other" has different abilities and talents that will empower you, but your other is only as good as you are if you are evil it will be evil, if you are good... Well you get the point" I walked up the long stairs, the light at the end of the tunnel came rushing towards me I was emerged in such great power I have never felt such bliss... Such peace.... Such serenity... Different animal spirits surrounded me as if I was in a world wind. It was large assortment of creatures varied in appearance and sizes. They circled around me even looking at me with piercing eyes observing me seeing if we connected as one. None of the spirits were my other; the strange animals went through my flesh-less body after they were done, and they abruptly stopped disappearing and fading away into the light.

Detriku appeared before me and said "You have been rejected by them... You cannot be the one... Maybe we were mistaken..." Detriku placed his hand on my chest "I will send you back to the tree of life" my body started to shake violently; it felt as if it was being torn into two directions. A black mist seeped out of me and from me I produced another being. "AHHH I can't take it what's happening to me" "Your other has always been with you... How could this be? The only way this is possible is if you already existed before this life"

Detriku then realized who I was and said "You are the savior of Zephyr!!!" He jumped around in excitement I was still uncomfortable with such a prestigious title of savior, if I truly was a savior how could I be dead? The black bird flew around over me, some of its feathers had gray on the tips and the end of his wings were red flame feathers that faded into the air.

I fell on my knees as if I ran a marathon, I was exhausted. I placed my hands on the ground then I lifted my head, we were back in the oasis. I looked at the very distinctive and dark colorful bird; he had a fiery intense look to his eyes. I got up and stood to my feet, I walked over to the bird and touched his head "do I look like a pet to you" it sharply spoke out. You speak "of course i speak what do you take me for an animal!?" I was perplexed because this loud mouth, rude, obnoxious bird was my other how could I be paired with such a character. "I am Scythe" he said.

Detriku interjected and said "Now that you have your other you now have the means to enter into the world of the living. Time here is slower and virtually non-existing unlike the world of the living so things might have change since your time here. When you get there you will need to learn the art of possession, you must find a body and enter it to be in the world of the living. "He waved his hand and magical orbs came out of his hands creating a portal of light. This was our conduit back to the world of the spirits and our way to get to Ka-bal, Scythe flew onto my shoulder and the portal consumed both Scythe and I. We were teleported back to the world of spirits.

Chapter 9

I recognized this place, it was the "Sanctuary of the fallen Kings" located on the out skirts of Bawurr before the Isona fields. Deeply rooted underground, the sanctuary was a monument that preserved the corpse of the great kings that had died. The only bodies left on Zephyr were Kings all other left to ascend up to Isara on the talus of magic. The area Scythe and I were in was a spacious catacomb with all of the fallen Kings many of them were slain by Ka-bal. All of them still in one piece (even Javos whose head was ripped off) not decayed or decrepit, they were preserved by great magic that kept their form intact.

"We need to find a body. Detriku said we have to learn the art of possession, otherwise we are useless in this form." Scythe said having his back facing me; we did not like each other very much something that shares a soul with me was certainly the complete opposite. "I don't know how to possess anyone, I've never done it" "well we have to learn fast we don't have much time contemplating how we are going to do it."

I turned around observing the many kings at rest, there arms folded with their crowns laid across their chest. I walked to the center of room where there were steps leading to a particular talus with a lights from the outside shinning on it. In the center of the room were steps leading to a secluded talus that radiated with an aurora of colors. I climbed the steps and approached the talus; my eyes widened and could not believe it. It was me, Scythe flew on my shoulder and looked down at my corpse, and it was oddly the only body that had no flesh but just bones that were still intact as if it was being stored for something. In scripted on the talus read "The fallen lord Reaven" who could have placed my body here? I was just a knight nothing more.

When I died my body was not only dismantled and ripped apart, but they set me on fire to ensure that I was dead. My hatred filled through my body, I clenched my hands tightly with fierce anger. "I will kill him" I said out loud Scythe felt everything I felt and vice versa, we were one whether we liked it or not. A couple of guards were walking by, Scythe said we need to be one with the host. I looked at him with confusion "What do you mean one with the host?" Scythe said "In order for us to get back to the world of the living, we need to find our first vessel to practice on"

The Sanctuary was heavily guarded, it was protected well. Not only did it have the fallen Kings but it was also the home of Agantus who was held deep within the cold mucky caves. I jumped down from the high place my body was on unto the ground; I was not sure how this works or what I should do to get inside a body. Walking up the guards who were talking about the Arena and that all the cities Murdrik, Sarianas, Tanali, Raka, Aknoli and Bawurr were all participating in the most famous event of blood, gore and death. Now that Ka-bal ruled over all the cities, I'm sure they were compelled to have more events since he was always entertained by gore and death.

The guards continued to talk to each other about the event; they were different since I left. There were various types of Zephyrians that were usually from other cities. Scythe turned to me and said "Now! Go and possess his body" I ran towards the guard and entered into him, we both struggled for a while. The guards next to him didn't know what was going on "Whats wrong with you?" they asked, we fell and hit the wall. The other 6 guards looked at us, while watching the black mist came off the guard's body. "Ka-bal told us to kill anything suspicious! we have to kill him" they formed up on me pulling out their swords.

I felt pressure coming from my back ripping and appeared a sword which was burred on my right side my shoulder. On my sides two chakrams misted, they were pure silver with three blades that connected them together similar to a Scythe blade forming a circle with some gaps in between. After being in the spirit world and Gregorie for so long I had forgotten how it is to be alive, to have my lungs filled with air and life. This was not a time to appreciate such luxury; the Guard to my right had electrical current surging through his hands.

I grabbed my sword and it spun in the air thrusting my body upwards them making a detrimental impact cutting his body from his neck down to the side of his hip. half his torso fell on the ground and began to sizzle as if he drank a class of acid, not only did my blade have ridged edges but is an effective in slicing through my enemies scorching them with a hot poisonous element that slowly burns the flesh of whoever it touches.

I took my chakrams and threw them both at the two guards running towards me, as soon as it touched them their bodies exploded and there remains painted the floor and some of the four other guards around them. They all had a look on their face of fear never seen such a powerful combatant, Ka-bal warned them I would arrive but forgot to tell them I could not be stopped. Obviously he didn't care. Scythe jumped into the body of the guard to my left, he used his electrical current to shock the head of the guard standing next to him. The guard's body convulsed until his eyes popped out causing him to burn in his metal armor. Scythe slammed both his hands on the ground conjuring up several sharp black blades that impaled the remaining two guards.

He was weak after this short encounter causing him to flop out of the body, he could only manipulate for short periods of time. The guard he possessed realized that all his guards were dead and quickly struck me with his sword cutting off my arm. I heard the soul of the Zephyrian inside me yell, although I didn't feel the pain he did. I swung my sword decapitating him and with one blow he was dead. This was our first fight together and wouldn't be out last, not until Ka-bal was dead.

Chapter 10

The blood from my severed arm ran down my body, I knew that it would not be long before I needed to find another host to sustain myself in the world of the living. Scythe turned to me and said "Now that you have this body we need to get up to Bawurr and find Ka-bal" We could have went through the caves but eventually we would run into the Agantus and he would have ripped this body to shreds instantly. We snuck past the heavily fortified catacomb and ascended up to the temple. Guards approached me and said "Navii are you okay? Your arm is gone" I told them "There is an intruder down stairs and he killed the rest of the guards" They gathered their weapons and ran down stairs to the catacomb, Scythe hid himself in the world of spirits until we made our way out side. Bawurr was just up ahead but I needed to find another body and soon.

I took my chakrams and slit my neck, the body dropped and I was back in the world of spirits. We continued to walk towards Bawurr, looking at it from a distance there was a certain darkness hovering over the land. I couldn't have been away that long for Zephyr to have changed so much. The land looked sick, as if it was polluted for decades. "This cannot be. There is something wrong" "yeah and its name is Ka-bal, well find out answers when we get to Bawurr" Scythe said.

I entered through the gates of Bawurr it seemed like everything was the same, the beautiful enormous city was exactly how it was when I left it. Besides the gray skies that surrounded it, Bawurr was still my home. Walking through the city brought back memories of me growing up, my parents, Lavina, and Tesious were all apart of my upbringing. Memories were so surreal I almost got lost in them. I needed to see her and tell her that I was still alive, well theoretically I was. "We have come back from the dead and your first priority is to visit a married Zephyra" I knew I could rely on Scythe to at least be honest with me even if he was rude.

I was growing tired of his blunt words so I lashed out saying "I don't see why you care your nothing but a insensitive bird without a heart or conscious" "If you forgot, you and I share the same soul we are no different I am just the more sensible one I guess I got the brains in the family" "AHH HOW DID I GET STUCK WITH YOU! YOU ARE NOT MY OTHER YOU ARE A MISTAKE!!!" "Well that makes two of us because I hate you already we have a planet to save and your fixated on a Zephyra when your no longer a Zephyro! YOUR DEAD IF YOU HAVEN'T notice, nothing but a user of bodies because you don't have one of your own!"

We both got silent letting the rage boil "Were going to see Tesious first! I have to know if shes okay! I'm going with or without you!" I walked away from Scythe before he could say another smart ass remark. Being an unseen outsider looking in, made me feel a sense of displacement as if I should have stayed dead and the world was better off without me. I observed the families together and the productivity of the shops and businesses, it made me appreciate what I no longer had. It was nostalgic, I recognize the exact place where Lavina and Vertic met and how he saved her life. Looking carefully, I noticed that the table was still a little broken from when the Kepler attacked Lavina years ago.

Before Tesious was taken from a servant girl in Bawurr city, her and I always use to talk about one day growing old together and always being friends. We wrote letters to each other all the time, even though we were young we always said were going to get married. I loved Tesious, the day she left I remember clearly. I was crushed because I knew things would never be the same, I mean how could it be? She was going to live with the king in a royal paradise while I was stuck in Bawurr city with nothing to offer her. The day she left I wrote her letter saying "Dear Tesious. I wish you all the happiness in the world and I wish you were not leaving but I know you have to. Being with you made me feel like I mattered in this world, you were my only real friend I have ever had and I will miss you every day. I promise I will write you all the time even if you forget about me, I hope you don't. I love you"

I wrote her for months after she left Bawurr, she never responded to my letters. So eventually I stopped trying to contact her thinking she forgot about me. Maybe she didn't feel the same about me like I did her, either way I couldn't continue reminiscing about the past, I had to see if she was okay. The last time I really saw her was when Lavina died, other than that she was always locked up in the castle. When we did see each other very little words were exchanged all but "Hello my Queen" or quick glance in each other's direction. We could never do much interaction between each other because Ka-bal would never allow it with anybody.

Indulging in the memories of my past was very time consuming but we eventually arrived at the front gate of Bawurr's castle. There were two guards standing outside. Walking by the guards reminded me of my time in under Ka-bal, I served with dignity and pride without any questioning. Their faces reflected passion I once had, if they only knew that their king didn't care about nothing or no one and was planning on destroying all life.

The castle was the tallest building in all of Bawurr, it had 100 levels with over 5,000 rooms. It had many buildings some levels floating and attaching to other buildings like a jigsaw puzzle. The moat made the castle very distinctive from the rest of the city; it was the heart of the city and also the life force of the magic that flowed throughout it. There were four bridges on all four sides of the beautiful castle that was well fortified.

This was not the time to get wrapped up in my thoughts and self-pity so I covered it up and concentrated on what needed to be done. "Come on" I said to Scythe still angry with him for being so cruel "wait" I stopped and turned back Scythe looked at me and said "The world would not be better without you" for the first time Scythe showed that he actually had a heart. "It seems the world would not be better off without the both of us, let's go"

Chapter 11

Going all the way up to the hundredth floor was a task all on its own; I did not want to possess anyone just yet because I knew Ka-bal already alerted his guards. Scythe and I trooped all the way to the top of the level going to the king's room. We were finally there, but I felt anxious proceeding. Watching the door for a couple of seconds wishing that time was kinder, I wanted to go back when Tesious and I were still in our youth playing under the three bright orange suns.

"Thank you Vallin" I heard a voice from the room speak, "My Queen, is there anything else I can get you. The Arena's event is beginning soon I presume King Ka-bal is expecting your arrival" "Yes I will only be a minute" The door opened and a servant walked out the room. Looking at him i knew this was my chance, Scythe said "We don't have much time you need to enter his body." I possessed him before he was about to turned the corner where there were guards approaching. This time it was not as bad considering he was not a fighter.

I opened the door and there was Tesious facing her mirror "I do not need anything else Vallin" I walked closer to her and she turned around "Is there something wrong?" Tesious turned around and I could not believe my eyes. She had aged over 500 years! Tesious was looking at me with eyes of confusion unsure why I was staring at her as if I had not seen her in forever. "You're just as beautiful as I remember" I said, Tesious squinted her eyes and slanted her head "Vallin... You're acting...." I interrupted her and said "You may not recognize me in this form... But it's me" we both paused and she completed my sentence "Reaven???" I smiled at her and she opened my arms and cried on my chest. "I had dreams you would come back to me... You... You... You have been away for 523 years"

I couldn't believe it, I was in Gregorie for a half a life time and my world and everything that I knew had changed drastically. "I don't have much time, Ka-bal is having an event in the Arena and I have to be present... I know what you are the Osawa told me everything... " "Tesious... I..." "Please we will have all the time in the world later but you have to stop what Ka-bal is doing... He is still killing innocent lives for sport and I can't bear to see it this time, he has young Zephyrian children and even parents fighting to feed their children. He plans on unleashing the Agantus and killing everyone." "I need a stronger body to fight the Agantus,""You need to possess a demon. My dreams showed me everything; they are the only ones that can stand up the Agantus. There is a demon in cell 194, I overheard Ka-bal saying that it is one of the strongest warriors and I was going to go up against Agantus"

Before I left I hugged Tesious and for a moment we were together again. I pressed my lips against hers and then said "Everything will be okay, I am going to kill Ka-bal and end this once and for all" "Ka-bal is setting up to break the seal between Gregorie and the world of the living if he does that then we are all dead" "I won't let that happen, I promise" "Before you go I just wanted you to know that I never stopped loving" her response was unexpected "I wrote you when we were kids but I guess you had forgot me" Tesious said. "I wrote you for months before I stopped trying" "You did?" "Yes! Considering our murderous King I'm sure he had everything to do with it!"

I quickly left the body and made my way down to the Arena. "Ohh... Umm... My Queen I apologize I don't remember coming into your room" "it's okay Vallin I am going to the Arena now please escorts me" There was a servant at the door watching her kiss Vallin "My lady are you okay? That's not King Ka-bal" "Yes I was just thanking Vallin for his service" Tesious was still memorized by the kiss but she knew she still had to make her way down to the Arena to sit by Ka-bals side. She had to keep her composure because she knew that if he knew that Reaven was back and she knew about it he would kill her. Ka-bal looked at his own wife as expendable. Her heart pounded and raced the beating of felt like she was stabbed in her chest. Her feelings for Reaven never changed after all this time, but she never got the chance to tell him how she felt.

Chapter 12

"IT IS TIME!" a loud voice echoed through the Arena. The announcer introduced the first contestants. Scythe and I went down to the underground passage were many contestants were preparing for battle. All including Zephyrians and an assortment of Demons. Ka- bal made his contestants stay in the cell for 3 days with minimal food and water so that their survival mode would kick in. That was his way to ensure that no one would forget the purpose of the sport, kill or be killed.

I looked through the cells, observing the vicious foul beast that was ready to rip each other to shreds. I remembered that Tesious said to look for cell 194, inside would be a demon that was almost as strong as Agantus. One of the last cells to the left held a regenerative demon made out of rock and stone, it was cell 194. This creature was swift, strong and my best bet to killing Agantus. I went through the bars of the cell, the thick bars going through my transparent body was a sensation that I couldn't get used to. Being an apparition was still new to me and I was still getting use to my new abilities. Shifting from both realms of spirit and living made me a god; still I didn't feel that way.

The creature made noises, groans and howls. He was eager to get out there and kill. I touched its body and it felt my presence causing it to suspiciously look around the area. Possessing a demon was going to be a lot different than a Zephyrian, their energy being so much greater than anything I have experienced. I jumped into the demon and felt the surge of power running through the both of us. The demon fought back with great might slamming into the walls of the cell and punching the floor, it screamed with fits of rage until it collapsed to the ground.

A guard came by to see what was going on, by then I was in complete control. Scythe influenced the guard allowing us to be the next fighter. The guard walked out to the announcer's cubicle "Hey...There is a demon wanting to fight Agantus" the guard said to the Announcer" "Well there's a show! Another victory for Agantus." he said with such enthusiasm "The king will be pleased". The Announcer walked to the center of the Arena "Zephyr!!! We were going to wait till the end but I think it's time to do it now... You know who the un-defeated champion is already" The crowds yelling got louder and louder "There's another un-defeated champion... From the city of Raka.... I-N-T-R-O-D-U-C-I-N-G!!! G-Y-P-H-R-O!!!"

My cell gate opened and the roaring crowd was uncontrollable. I stepped out into the Arena Scythe flew on my shoulder "This is our chance to fight Agantus, if we win, Ka-bal won't have anything to stop us "My plan exactly!" My eyes were filled with rage anticipating my revenge so Ka-bal would finally get what he deserves; this was my chance to make him suffer as I had suffered.

Tesious sat by his side holding his hand, I looked over at them and that fueled my hatred even more. He has taken everything from me and I wanted him dead. The mage's with their extraordinary magic released all the seals that kept Agantus in his tomb. The announcer started stirring the excitement of the crowd "This is it.. THE MOMENT YOU ALL HAVE BEEN WAITING FOR... TWO UNDEFEATED TITANS FIGHTING TO THE DEATH!!! WHO WILL WIN???"

As much power that I had I was still uncertain of my full potential, I was still a virgin to my own abilities. Seven mage's took off the binding magic that concealed Agantus, he climbed out the cave and jumped into the air creating a mini quake indenting the ground. His momentum once his feet touched the ground caused a powerful quake, everything shook and the crowd once again went wild. This body was not even half the size of him; I almost reached his knees but just berley.

"How are we going to fight him?" I ask Scythe "How the hell should I know" he simply replied. Agantus ran towards us stomping and breathing heavily, I jumped out the way before he used his enormous hand clashing into the ground. I threw my chakrams at his face and he lifted his hands trying to block them. The chakrams went through his hands macing him to howl loudly. I grabbed my sword and charged at him he swung his arm at the ground and I used his arm as a leverage to get closer to his face.

I ran up his arm and he opened his mouths trying to devour my body. I flipped past his jaws and pierced his eye with my sword, the crowd was silent because they never seen a combatant go up against Agantus lasting this long or even came close to severely hurting him. Scythe turned into multiple blades that levitated, he charged through his body effortlessly, Agantus fell on his back and lay before me. Agantus got up but was still disoriented from the devastating blow; I was ready for his next move.

My hands started to produce mist from it granting me the ability to telekinetically manipulate my surroundings. I used my new telekinetic abilities to send out a force wave that hit his pelvic causing him to crouch down to the floor, Scythe flew into the ground and two shackles wrapped around Agantus arms. The tightness from Scythe shackles caused Agantus hands to bleed; Scythe moved the shackles through the ground so Agantus would fall forward. I saw his body coming down so I created a mystic blade that ripped through the ground ripping through his head. Agantus brains exploded out of his thick skull, the sudden trauma caused Agantus to shake for a moment. His arms and legs began to flap around until his body completely stopped moving, the poison from his mouth flowed down his body it began to melt.

Ka- bal got up and the crowd thought he was pleased so they began to chant and cheer "S-I-L-E-N-C-E!!!" the crowd quieted quickly "He killed Agantus!!! This is the first time ever!" Ka-bal did not know if to be pleased or filled with passionate anger. "No one faces the Agantus and wins" Tesious face was full of happiness she almost got up and started cheering for me, but she remembered that Ka-bal was right next to her.

I knew that he knew who I was and that I was back to kill him. "Gyphro is a murderer! Let all the contestants out and kill him!" Ka-bal said, Every cell opened up from every direction all the challengers came out. "We need to leave now" Scythe said the gates opened and all of the challengers focused their attention on killing Gyphro. I left the Gyphro body; he was weak from the energy I had used from him. The gated warriors attacked Gyphro hitting him for every direction repeatedly. Gyphro could not defend himself, the whole Arena became a battlefield leaving nothing but a pool of blood and severed limbs.

Chapter 13

As soon as I exited Gyphro's body time froze and the world of the living deteriorated fading before my eyes. I found myself back in front of the Tree of life "So you have passed your first test" "I don't remember being proctored like a school child" I sarcastically added "You defeated Agantus which showed me your strength and you are very tactful" "I passed your test now let me back to Bawurr to face Ka-bal" "There are still two things left... Wisdom and Compassion" "I have no time for your games. I need to find Ka-bal and..."

Before I got to finish I was transported to my old home in Bawurr. I was young again, when I was only 30 years old which meant I was still a child. Mom and dad were exactly how I remembered them, Mom cooking in the kitchen and Dad reading his books of the universe. "Foods almost ready" Mom said, Lavina came out from her room and started preparing the table. Dad came and sat at the head of the large square table that was held up by magic.
Mom made my favorite dish Crommy stew; it was a type of fish that even after it is cooked it still moves. It was delicious, mom always made the tentacles so it would move outside of the plate because she knew how much I loved playing with it before I ate it. She always made sure I had at least three eye balls in the middle of the plate because I loved them.

Things were perfect just as I remembered them to be Dad looked at me and said "You know you don't have to go back son" Mom followed his statement saying "The world does not need you like we do, we love you"

I looked up at them and said "But I am supposed to do something but I can't remember what it is" Lavina said "Well it must have not been that important if you easily forgot" "Yeah your probably right... It couldn't be that important"

We all continued to eat but I couldn't shake off what I had to do, it was as if my short term memory was completely erased. I knew my family was dead but all this seemed so real, maybe I had a second chance at life maybe this is where I belonged. "Would you like to play with Tesious maybe tomorrow we will invite her over for dinner as well" my mother said "yeah I would like that" I replied. Lavina poked fun at me saying that I was in love with her and we how mushy I got when she was around.

Suddenly there was a tapping at the window, I got out of my seat and looked out and saw a bird looking in. I stared into its eyes for a while trying to remember where I saw it before.
and my purpose started to come back to me, I had to save Zephyr! My temporary amnesia didn't distract me for long. I looked down at the floor not paying attention to anything in particular just letting my mind wonder outside the realm of logic. I turned over to the table and they were all sitting there lifeless. The table was filled with blood and maggots eating away at their

flesh, it occurred to me that my family has been dead for hundreds of years
"What kind of sorcery is this" this display of my family's corpses was disturbing.

I was still a child and my emotions still came into effect, I ran towards them and screamed "Moooommmm!!! Daaaadddd!!! Laviiiiinnnaa!!!" then my Mom snapped her neck back in place and said "You can bring us back all you have to do is stay" her voice was dark and she spoke in an unknown tone as if it was something speaking out of her. My father with his head on the table looked up at me and said "Your destiny is with us son... There is nothing out there for you" the house began to shake and the floors cracked open as if there was a quake going on. My knees buckled unto the ground, I did not have enough strength considering I was younger and weaker.

Looking over at Lavina her chest was ripped apart and her legs were not attached to her body and her hand was bitten off exactly how she had died. "End the pain Reaven... End it now!!! I need you, we need you" she said "But you told me to go back and save Zephyr when you were in Gregorie" "The pain is too much, It hurts!!! Please Reaven" she took her final breath and sat on the chair lifeless. "Noooo!!!" I yelled Scythe broke through the window and landed on the floor "We need to leave this place its playing tricks on your mind"

"Maybe this is where I belong" "You are foolish if you think this your family!!! They are dead!!! Now remember who you are! and lets get out of here!" Scythe flew on my shoulder "Your right"

My youth was gone and I was back to my original self again. "This had to be the test of wisdom". I knew it was "Yeah a few moments ago you were about to mess up everything and stay here with the walking dead" "thanks I knew I could always count on you for your understanding and comforting words." "Anytime" we were both relieved it was over. I opened the door prying it open, nothing but darkness was visible but I walked through it anyways.

Chapter 14

The Darkness evolved as I continued to walk through it. Scythe and I were now back in a familiar place, Pierce Kod. I remembered these caves very well; it was the last time that I still alive before Ka-bal crushed everyone in my body sending me head first into Gregorie. Walking through the wondrous cave the images began to appear once again, but this time it wasn't any of my memories. I walked closer to the cave walls and marveled at all it was showing me. Ka-bal was talking to Nexius saying "Tesious will die tonight, her time has come to open the Orb of Tesik" "Yes my lord have you not told her that she isn't even real? Her whole life was a lie shes nothing but a key to unlocking the spirit world" "She will find out soon enough but for now the less she knows the better. I dont want to have to kill her prematurely."

This could not be real! Tesious was part of Ka-bals plan all these years! I continued to listen to Nexuis "My lord we only have one chance at this the next time all the suns and moon line up perfectly will be in 500 years! If not done at the exact time it will put a tamper on our plans preventing your immortality." Ka-bal clenched his teeth and squeezed his hand "You told me that you saw Reaven resurrected back from Gregorie! He will try and save her Im sure of it!" "Yes my lord but he had help. It seems that Strovos and

Faeus decided to betray us! But he cannot stop you my lord once you obtain your "other" you will be unstoppable, and you can then banish him for all eternity" The walls faded, I could not hear anymore "What did they mean by banished?" Scythe said "we are obviously seeing this so we can prevent it from happening! We have to go after Nexius, he is going to kill Tesious. If that happens we are going to have more than Ka-bal to worry about!" "Your right we need to move faster we cannot let him get to Tesious"

My name was being called "R-E-A-V-E-N" in such a sweet and soft tone. I walked into the Osawa's sanctuary and there they were waiting for me. The Osawa's eyes circled around me as it did in our first encounter. The eyes emerged with one another, their radiance illuminated the cave making this damp and unpleasant place a serene paradise. The pupil of the eyes created a white light and a figure formed from it. The naked figure began to descend downward levitating getting closer to me. The shadow became more recognizable.
I walked closer, and she began to speak "I am the Lady of the eye. Reaven, It is time for you to fulfill your destiny and make your choice for which path you want to be on" "What do you mean which path? You speak as if I have a choice in this entanglement." The lady of the eye extended her hands and created two talus's, one of which showed Zephyr and the salvation it would

receive if I saved it. The second was of my family and Tesious, all of them were standing there before Ka-bal had taken them all from me.

The lady of the eye said "It is time to complete your final test of Compassion, will you choose to forget everything and go back to your life where Ka-bal never existed or will you choose to fulfill your destiny and save Zephyr... Be warned that both paths have its consequences. " I was pleased with that path, a world without Ka-bal would be better. I said to her "If I go back to my family and Ka-bal never existed then the world would not need to be saved" The lady of the eye said "In that world yes, you will grow old and live a happy life, but this world would inevitably be destroyed creating a disruption in the time line, Eventually your world will parish sooner or later."

Watching my life through the talus was a true glimpse of Isara, the feeling of belonging and being normal was what I have been longing for after my parents had died and the events that lead to the tragic deaths of Vertic and Lavina. I walked to up to the holographic image of my family, I was happy and Tesious and I were together with children of our own. How could I renounce this opportunity of pure happiness? Scythe said "I know your heart. I would understand if you decide to forget this and get them back. You have had so much taken from you; it would be selfish if I asked you to deny it."

I grabbed Tesious hand and said "I have loved you since we were children and my heart will always be intertwined with yours" Lavina was next to her and said "Choose to stay with us Reaven...This is where you belong" Scythe put his head down because he knew what I wanted to do. I looked at the Lady of the eye and said "I have made my decision... I will fulfill my destiny and will save both Zephyr and Isara!" "You have chosen well" the talus that showed my alternate world sunk into the ground sucking in my parents and Tesious, they began to scream as the fire burned them alive and hands came out pulling them into the abyss. Lavina lashed out of the talus, her face turned into a something demonic. Her fingers grew long and she started clawing me "How could you choose the world over us! I hate you and you will die by Ka-bals hand just as we did!" I grabbed her hands and kicked her off of me causing her to fall in to the abyss. She screamed as the hands pulled her down and the hot flames started to turn her to ashes. "You will die savior!" she began to laugh as the talus closed in the ground.

"That wasn't your sister" Scythe said "I know it was another test of my will, nothing will stop me from killing Ka-bal" The lady of the eye looked at me "now that you have chosen your path, it is time for you to go back and stop Ka-bal from opening the Orb of Tesik! For you to be strong enough to do so I'll tell you this, the power resides in your bones, seek them and they will sustain you and make you whole. All will be revealed to you but now you have to go back" I looked at the Lady of the eye and said "I don't understand I don't know what you mean!" "Time is not on your side" she said as she sent me back to Bawurr.

Chapter 15

I was back in Zephyr, this time I am coming for both Nexius and Ka-bal. Since Nexius was Ka-bal's strongest defense and I need to go after him first so that he would have no one to hide behind. I knew where to find him; he rarely left the chambers in the castle. He was the one that would kill Tesious but not if I killed him first. Scythe and I were prepared for our final battle we knew what we had to do and how to do it. We went to Nexius tower, there were 2 guards walking down the steps I possessed one of them. Scythe manipulated the other guard causing him to run off the steps and wall from the stair case his body hit the sides and exploded on his impact to the ground. I opened the door to Nexius room, there was smoke covering the whole room making it hard to see. I walked through the mist extracting my sword from my back; I grabbed one chakram and tried to listen carefully to see if I could catch him by surprise.

A bolt of electrical current blew me back to the other side of the room smashing me into a pillar that ran through the middle of the room. I got back on my feet and threw my chakram in the direction of the bolt I knew it had missed because I heard it clash against the wall "Nexius!!!! You hide out of your own fear!!! YOU KILLED EVERYONE I LOVED AND NOW YOU ARE THE ONE WHO IS AFFRAID OF DEATH!!!" Nexius showed himself and said "You are a stupid boy for coming here! Ka-bal will use the Orb of Tesik and will be the god of this world" "He is going to kill Tesious!!!" "Yes he will, she holds the key to opening the conduit of this world to the essence of fate, it was always her we needed!" From behind me Nexius said "It already begun" he had divided himself up there were 20 or maybe even 30 of him surrounded me.

I jumped in the air stabbing his body, I cut off the clone to my left head as it flew in the air I spun and kicked it knocking the clone behind me out cold. I grabbed my other chakram and threw it at a table which had potions and magic. The combination caused it to combust explode; the explosion was so massive it broke through the floor and buried some of the clones. Scythe manipulated one them and used their magic to create a spiraling orb vortex that sucked some of them in, crushing and devouring their bodies. Scythe flew to the window and said "The place is going to explode come on!" before I left I spotted the real Nexius he was laying on the ground, it had to be him "This is for what you did my sister" I lunged my fist into his chest moving passing his bones and ripping out his heart, as I pulled it out I crushed it and it turned into stone crumbling into pieces. I didn't have much time to watch him suffer so I ran towards the window and jumped out. Falling from the great heights the explosion pushed me far away from the castle causing me to fall face forward into the ground. The explosion radiated outwardly then imploded vanishing much of the castle. I was back in the world of spirits, I looked down and saw the corpse of the guard I possessed head was bent all the way back touching his back as if he had opisthotonos and his stomach was opened exposing his organs.

I knew I had to find Ka-bal and fast, even though he did not have Nexius anymore that would have never stopped him from trying to completing the ritual. There was only one place that I knew that Ka-bal would have gone, that would have been to the Sanctuary of the fallen kings. That is where I saw him conversing with Nexius about the "The orb of Tesik" since he was gone, im sure the events have now changed, how much though I did not know. I ran out of the city of Bawurr, Scythe flew over me in the sky to see if he saw Ka-bal, but there was no trace of Ka-bal. "Wait I see something" beyond the city of Bawurr was a beaming light that shot straight to the sky, it was coming from the Sanctuary.

Exiting from the gates of Bawurr I could see clearly the Sanctuary. It was quite a distance away so I ran towards it. When we arrived at The Sanctuary of the fallen kings it was fortified heavily with guards. Hovering over it like a protective shell. I walked towards it and touched it, the shock threw me back soaring to the ground. If I was alive the force would have been devastating, I got up immediately. "There is a spell that prevents us from entering the sanctuary even in the spirit realm we cannot enter" Scythe said. All of the guards are inside the sanctuary so how could I get in? Scythe looked at me and said "maybe if we manipulate one of the travelers it won't be able to detect us" "I don't want to put innocent lives in danger.

It's too risky" he replied "we have to act fast or Tesious will die"

Some travelers were passing by taking some supplies in a carriage moved by two orange colored Laknics. Laknics were quick on their feet, they were medium sized that had four spring-like legs that helped them hop and leap to get to where they wanted. Many poorer citizens of the lower sides of Bawurr used them for labor after they had tamed them. Scythe manipulated one of them to jump out the carriage and set it on fire, eight guards came out to see what had happened probing the area. As soon as they crossed over I possessed the first guard, he had a large axe that I used to cut the legs off the guard next to him. I threw the axe in between the other guard's eyes cracking his skull wide open. The other six were surrounding me, Scythe jumped into the fire from the carriage and it became a large ball of fire. He ascended to the air and thew it to the ground turning the guards into ashes.

I walked over to the protective field and tried putting my hand through it, I quickly retracted it once I saw it was burning the skin of my new body. "This might work if we move fast enough" Scythe hid in my body as well, and we ran straight into the magical field. As soon as we entered it the body we possessed began to start to burn and his flesh began to dissolve, our legs were weak as we struggled to get through it. The burning was like acid, the soul inside me screamed in agony as we continued to walk through it "I am sorry, but this is the only way" I said to the spirit of the possessed. We were almost at the end but the body was weakening quickly as soon as we reached the end of the protective field the body disintegrated and we were forced out the body. The magical force threw us to the other side, I wondered to my self "who else did Ka-bal have that could generate such magic?"

We were finally here, our final moments before we would face Ka-bal. I was anxious; I wanted all my answers now! Entering the Sanctuary, it was dark and lit by flames that were mounted on the wall. Two of Nexius's mages were chanting holding hands; since they were under him I am sure they were almost as strong hence answering my questions about the protective field. "Those mages have great power, we could use that against Ka-bal" Scythe said "Your right let's do it" I took over one of the mages, it fought me with greater strength then any of the guards I had possessed before. The other mage cultivated a blizzard that began freezing the walls and the floor, Scythe manipulated his arm and made him touch his stomach turning him into a block of ice.

I didn't want to attract attention from the other guards that were lurking around. I vanquished all evidence of the ice and the mage making them disappear. "Are you ready?" I said to Scythe "You don't even have to ask! Let's get this bastard!" we descended down the spiraling steps, from afar we could hear faint voices. "Ka-bal!" I whispered to myself as we walked into the sanctuary I saw Tesious subdued with her hand hanging from magical shackles that kept her body levitated. She was unconscious, Ka-bal stood there next to her. There was a huge portal that was behind them "KA-BAL!!!" I screamed "You have no one to hide behind now!!! Nexius is dead!!!" "Hide behind?" he laughed a wicked laugh. Nexius appeared from behind him and said "You really think that you could kill me so easily? Those were just my servants and they handled you long enough for us to complete the ritual" "What!!!???" I jumped back in astonishment.

Ka-bal said "Let us begin" Tesious opened her eyes and was dazed at whatever they had done to her "Reaven..." she said my name wearily "NO!!! Tesious!!!" Ka-bal ripped her skin from her body and a pure white light radiated from her, where normally it would be blood and bones. I ran towards them but Nexius threw me against the wall with a binding spell. I could't move but only watch as Ka-bal placing his hand inside her back taking ripping a powerful orb from her. Her body started to break away and fell a part, Nexius held one hand towards me and the other facing the portal "Throw the orb inside my lord" Ka-bal threw the orb into the portal that then turned into flames. Nexius spoke into the portal saying "Great Detriku we call you for your power, release the spirits of the others" Ka-bals body was being drawn inside the portal, out of it came a large three headed beast with sharp fangs and paws. Its spinal cord was viable as the rest of its bones were through the exterior of the body.This creature was more intimidating than any other beast I had ever seen.

Ka-bal emerged with the other, as I watched the two become one being I knew I was to late. He was immortal and there was no way I could stop him. No Zephyrian on the planet could match him which meant my gift of possession was useless. His face had black veins, his whole appearance was darker and he visibly was bigger and stronger within seconds. Ka-bal no longer needed Nexius to conjure magic, He raised his hands and from it wind started blowing hard. Bolts of light were at his finger tips he threw them and it shocked my body. He continued until I was on the ground, this body was not strong enough to sustain attacks like that. I felt myself almost drifting in the world of spirits, "This is the end!!!" Ka-bal said in an evil voice as he used the shadows to form a long blade that flew straight into my chest. I tried to hold on as long as could but my body could not sustain anymore infliction.

When I awoke the place was deserted, Scythe was laid next to me. I nudged him and he lifted his head "You okay?" I said to Scythe "yeah but that last hit hurt!" "I know, I don't know how we are going to fight him, he used the orb of Tesik and now he's immortal" as soon as I said that the talus where my bones laid were glowing. I walked over to them and felt a strange sensation, Scythe flew on the talus next to the bones and said "Do you think this is what the lady of the eye meant by seeking the bones?"

I looked at the bones and knew that I had to possess them. Only then would I be able to fight Ka-bal. I looked back at everything he had taken from me, Vertic, Lavina, my parents and Tesious. The indescribable torment he bestowed on me was unforgivable. I touched the bones and felt the power of a true god. If I reconnected with my body, then I would be whole once more. I have had many deaths and many lives, but my resurrection would bring forth things I still didn't understand. All I did know is my resurrection was the key to my vengeance...

and my REDEMPTION....

(To be continued)....

About the Author

New York native Michael Victor King has been writing since he was 6 years old. In 2012 he decided to write his first book from all the creative dreams he was having. In March 2012 he started working on the development of the Reaven series. By October 2012 he began to write and complete it. Help raising his 2 nieces and working at many dead end jobs he decided to share his gift with the world. Still a young writer, Michael will soon branch off to many different genres in hopes to touch many different audiences.

If you enjoyed this book please rate and comment it.

Email: OfficialMVK@Gmail.com